Bess & Jodorowsky

SON OF THE GUN

#1 BORN IN THE TRASH

Humanoids Publishing™

To Teo

www.humanoids-publishing.com

Translation by Justin Kelly

Graphic design : Thierry Frissen

SON OF THE GUN: BORN IN THE TRASH

English language edition © 2001 Humanoids Inc. Los Angeles, CA, USA.
All rights reserved.

Humanoids Publishing
PO Box 931658
Hollywood, CA 90093

Printed in Belgium. Bound in France.

ISBN : 1-930652-51-8

Humanoids Publishing™ and the Humanoids Publishing logo are trademarks of:
Les Humanoïdes Associés S.A., Geneva (Switzerland)
registered in various categories and countries.
Humanoids Publishing, a division of Humanoids Group.

"THE DUST WHIRLS IN THE AIR, THEN SETTLES ON THE EARTH..."

"WHERE DO WE EARTH-BOUND TRAVELERS GO?"

"WE BRING THE CHRIST OF TLACAHUEPAN TO HIS DEATH..."

"THE SHOUTING DIES DOWN..."

"THE EARTH CRUMBLES, THE FLOWERS ROT AWAY..."

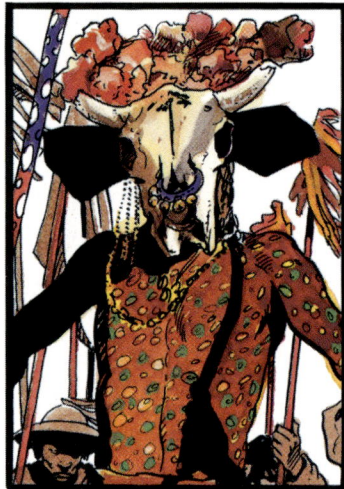

"I SPREAD MY WINGS, AND SHED TEARS BEFORE MY PEOPLE..."

"THE DUST WHIRLS IN THE AIR, THEN SETTLES ON THE EARTH..."

"WHERE DO WE EARTH-BOUND TRAVELERS GO?"

"WE BRING THE CHRIST OF TLACAHUEPAN TO HIS DEATH..."

MIDNIGHT... THE SIRENS SHRIEK IN THE DARKEST HOUR OF NIGHT... CURFEW...
KEEP RUNNING, MORONS!
MOVE YOUR ASSES!
WHEN THE SIREN STOPS, WE SHOOT!
QUICK! INTO THE CHURCH!
THEY'RE GOING TO SHOOT US!
LET ME THROUGH!
YOU CAN'T COME IN HERE!
DIRTY HOMOSEXUAL! AND A TRANSVESTITE, TOO!
BEGONE FROM THE HOUSE OF THE LORD, BASE CREATURE!
¡HIJO DE PUTA!
TRATA-TA-TATATATA

HOLY MARY MOTHER OF WHORES!

WHAT AM I SUPPOSED TO DO WITH YOU?

...IF I SAVE YOU, THE DOGS GO HUNGRY... WITH THE LIFE YOU'RE BEING BORN INTO, IT'S BETTER IF THEY DEVOUR YOU RIGHT AWAY...

HERE, LITTLE PUPPIES! COME AND GET YOUR TREAT

OH...

NOW I SEE WHY THEY THREW YOU AWAY...

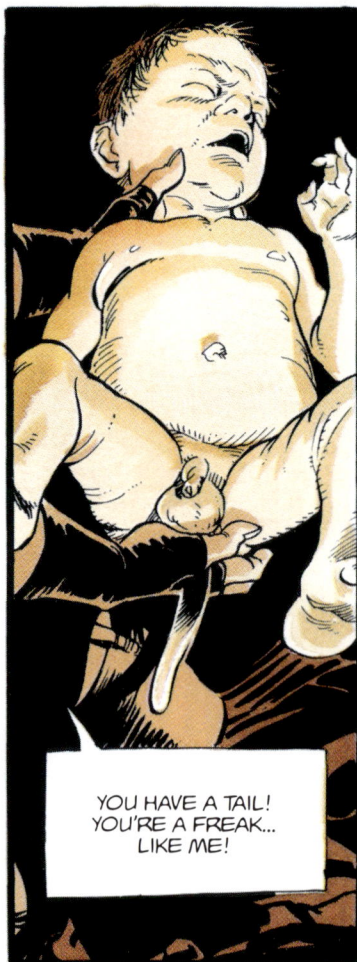

YOU HAVE A TAIL! YOU'RE A FREAK... LIKE ME!

16

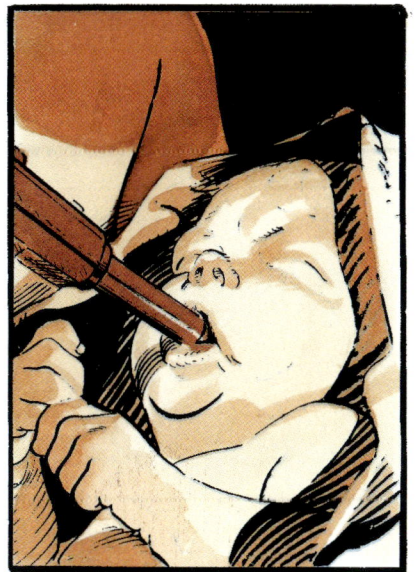

YES! YOU ABANDONED ME, AND I WAS RAISED ON DOG'S MILK!

SO NOW HEAR MY BARK...

MAKE IT RAIN! DO NOT ABANDON YOUR CHILDREN!

REMEMBER HOW YOU SPURNED MY MOTHER, THE DWARF... BUT HE FORCED YOU TO ACCEPT HIM...

HALF-PINT BROKE DOWN THE CHURCH DOORS! AND HE WAS RIGHT!

YOU ONLY LISTEN TO RAPE

WHERE'S YOUR CASH, QUEERIE?

YOU MUST KEEP A STASH SOMEWHERE!

THANKS AGAIN, SWEETHEART!

JUA... JUANITO...

COME CLOSE... I CAN'T MOVE...

HALF-PINT!

...THE BASTARDS BROKE MY BONES...

HOLD ON TO ME, II'LL HELP YOU UP...

NO POINT, JUANITO...

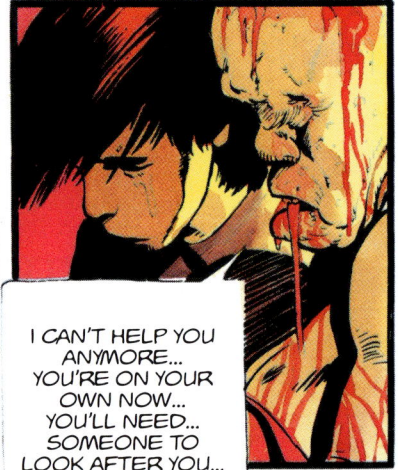

I CAN'T HELP YOU ANYMORE... YOU'RE ON YOUR OWN NOW... YOU'LL NEED... SOMEONE TO LOOK AFTER YOU...

CAREFUL... IT'S LOADED...

TEACH IT TO SPEAK... AND EVERYONE WILL RESPECT YOU...

NOW, HELP ME INTO THE CART...

...I HAVE A FRIEND... WHO'LL NEVER LET YOU DOWN... NO MATTER WHAT... INSIDE THE DOLL...

!

21

HALF-PINT!...

TELL ME, O LORD...
WHAT COULD HE HAVE
DONE TO DESERVE
SUCH A FATE?

I DON'T BELIEVE IT!
HE'S GOT A DOG'S TAIL!
LET'S MAKE HIM BARK...
BARK, YOU DIRTY DOG!
ARF, ARF! FETCH THIS ROCK, WOOF-WOOF!
YEAH, FETCH!
POK!
OWW!
THAT'S... THAT'S ENOUGH!
UH OH! HE'S GOING TO BITE!
LOOK OUT... IT'S A MAD DOG! ARF!

ON YOUR KNEES!

I COULD HAVE KILLED ALL OF YOU LIKE I KILLED THIS HORSE, AND DIPPED MY HAND IN YOUR BLOOD!

FROM NOW ON, YOU BELONG TO ME!

UNDERSTAND?!...

WE UNDERSTAND... YOU'RE OUR LEADER...

YOU'LL DO EVERYTHING I SAY?

YES...

AND THEN...

FINE... TONIGHT WE ROB THE OLD WOMAN SELLING TORTILLAS... WE KEEP ON ROBBING TILL WE HAVE ENOUGH TO BUY... A CAR!

EASY NOW... SLOW DOWN, ORLANDO...

THAT ONE? THE LOTTERY TICKET GIRL?

GO IN CLOSER... I WANT HER...

EL REY DEL

23

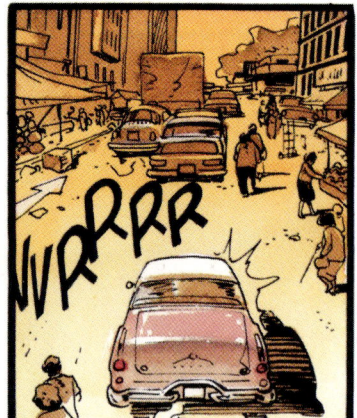

GET IN THE CAR, GUAPITA... YOU'RE GOING FOR A RIDE!

BUT!!? ARE YOU CRAZY?? LET GO OF ME!

LET ME OUT!

STEP ON IT, ORLANDO!

NOOO! HELP!!

UGGHH!

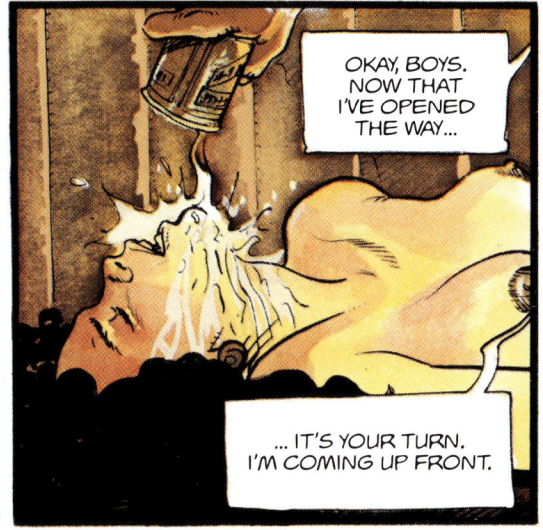

OKAY, BOYS. NOW THAT I'VE OPENED THE WAY...

... IT'S YOUR TURN. I'M COMING UP FRONT.

WAAOOH!...

WH... NO!! STOP!

NOOO!

FARTHER DOWN THE ROAD...

SCREEEEKKKRK

SCREEEEEK

TWELVE MORE BEERS FOR YOU GUYS! THAT MAKES TWO DOZEN!

TWENTY-FOUR BEERS... TWENTY-FOUR GIRLS...

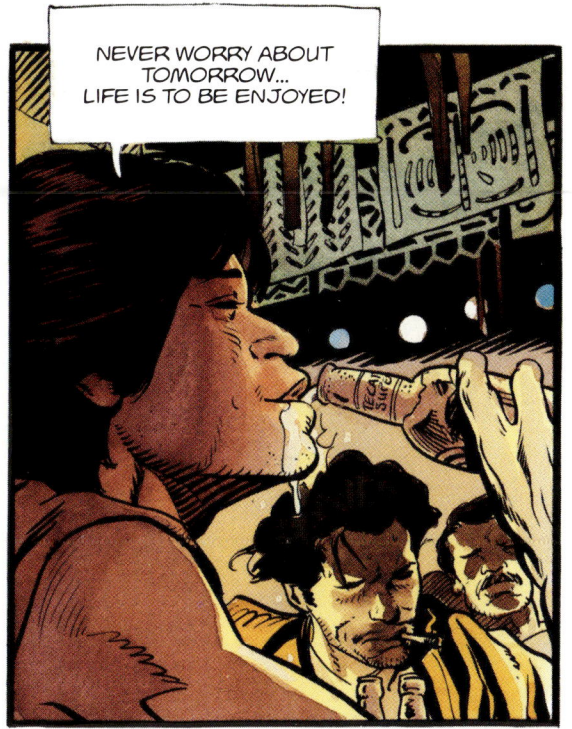

NEVER WORRY ABOUT TOMORROW... LIFE IS TO BE ENJOYED!

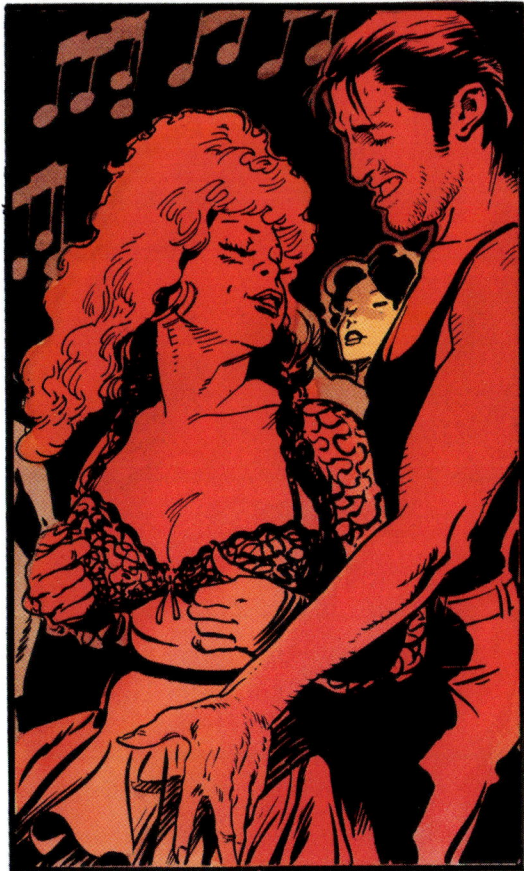

I HATE THIS GAY MUSIC...

...AND I HATE WATCHING GAY GUYS...

SHUT THAT VIOLIN UP!

...WRIGGLE THEIR BUTTS LIKE MONKEYS!

SO IS IT TRUE WHAT THEY SAY...

...YOU GOT A TAIL?

HERE IT IS... COME TAKE IT OFF...

...IF YOU'RE MAN ENOUGH!

KLICK

TAKE IT OFF...? YEAH, I'LL CUT IT OFF...

ARGGGGGGH!

TCHACK

UHH

KLICK!

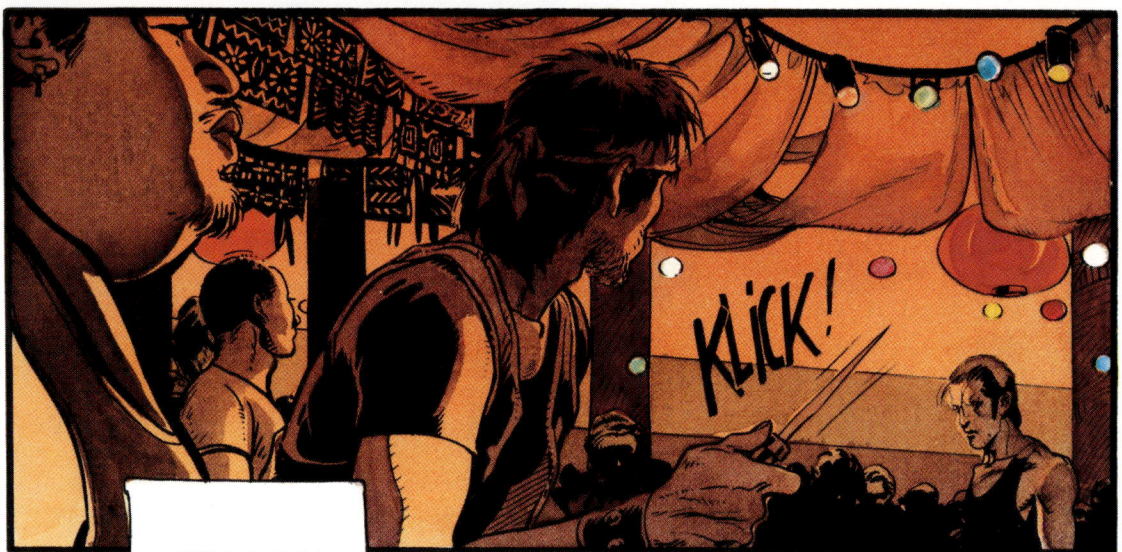

WE'LL SMASH
YOUR SKULL,
FREAK!

AAAAAAAA

TCHOCK

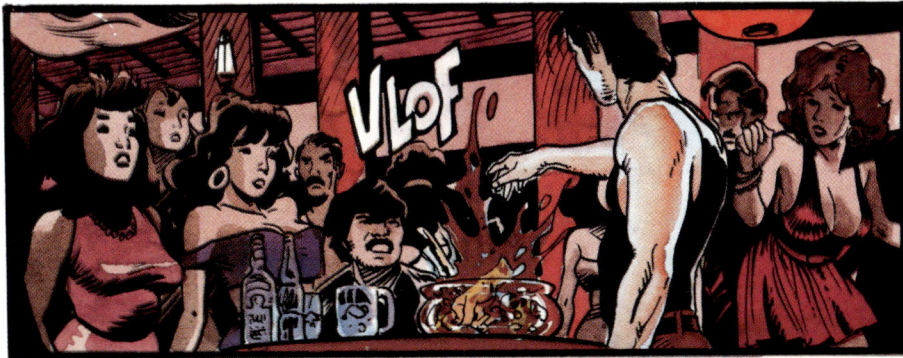

HEY, THAT QUACK LIVES IN OUR NEIGHBORHOOD...
WE COULD SNATCH HIM,
MAKE HIM DRAW US A DIAGRAM OF THE HOUSE...

JUST IMAGINE
ALL THE LOOT
INSIDE!

WHAT DO YOU THINK,
JUAN?

NOT BAD... BUT TOO RISKY...
I HAVE A BETTER IDEA...

WHEN THE DOC LEAVES
HIS HOUSE, YOU THREE
JUMP HIM AND
ROUGH HIM UP...
AND THAT'S
WHEN I COME IN!

...I SLAP YOU AROUND
A LITTLE BIT
AND DISARM YOU...
THEN YOU RUN AWAY,
AND I MAKE FRIENDS
WITH THE DOCTOR,
WHO INTRODUCES
ME TO THE P.M.

...THEN THE P.M. GIVES ME A
JOB... AND WHEN THE TIME
IS RIGHT, I OPEN THE DOOR
FOR YOU, AND... WE'RE IN!

ARE YOU GUYS
WITH ME?

YEAH, I'M
WITH YOU!

ME TOO, MAN...
WE'RE GONNA
GET RICH!

WE'LL DO IT JUST
LIKE YOU SAID,
JUANITO. YOU'RE
A GENIUS!

LET'S DO IT!

GIVE US YOUR WALLET, MAN! YOUR WATCH, TOO!

WHAT IS THIS? LET ME G...

HEY, YOU...

COUGH IT UP!

YOU'RE A LUCKY MAN... WE'RE NOT GOING TO SLIT YOUR THROAT... JUST YOUR BALLS!

DROP YOUR PANTS!

HEAR THAT, OLD GEEZER? YOU SHOULDN'T UPSET COCO!

FUCK

AAARGH

YOU'RE CRAZY! HELP! HELP ME!

HE'S PUTTING UP A FIGHT! WE'LL TEACH YOU TO ACT TOUGH! TAKE THAT!

IT'S OVER! I'LL HELP YOU UP...

!....

YOU'RE LUCKY I WAS PASSING BY...

YOU SAVED MY LIFE!

THOSE YOUNG PUNKS WERE GOING TO... CASTRATE ME! HOW HORRIBLE!

HOW CAN I EVER REPAY YOU?

REPAY ME?

WELL, SINCE YOU MENTION IT...

THE GOOD DOCTOR
ESCULAPE TOLD ME
THE WHOLE STORY.

YOU MANAGED TO DEFEAT
THREE HOOLIGANS USING
ONLY THIS OLD PISTOL...

YOU MIGHT NEED A MORE EFFICIENT
WEAPON NOW... STEP OVER HERE, AND
CHOOSE ANY ONE YOU WISH...

I'M LOYAL...
I'D RATHER
STICK WITH
MY OWN!

GO AHEAD,
TAKE ONE.

TAKE IT EASY,
ELDER...
EVERYTHING'S FINE...
OUR FRIEND IS
JUST A LITTLE
SPIRITED,
THAT'S ALL! PUT
AWAY YOUR GUN!

I LIKE WHAT YOU SAID ABOUT
LOYAL... AND WHAT'S TRUE FOR
THE GUN IS TRUE FOR OTHER
THINGS, RIGHT?

HOW FAR CAN I
TRUST YOUR LOYALTY?

THAT'S GOOD,
VERY GOOD... NOW WE'LL
PUT YOU TO THE TEST...
I NORMALLY KEEP TWELVE
BODYGUARDS...
YOU CAME JUST IN TIME...

UNTIL DEATH, UNLESS I'M
BETRAYED...

37

41

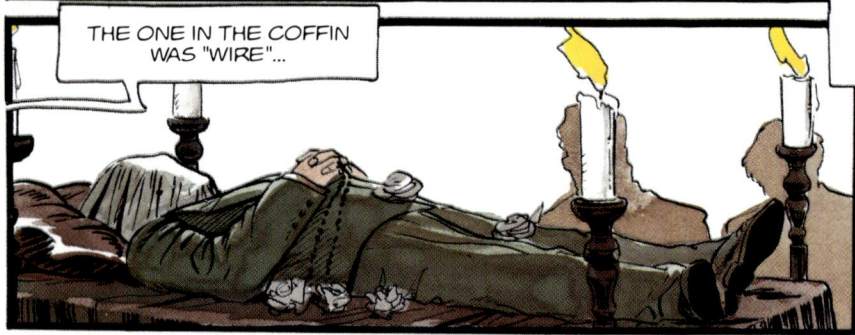

...PINOCCHIO"...

..."THE GREEK"...

..."CYCLOPS"...

...I'M "BIGMOUTH"...

...AND "TUTTI FRUTTI". AT YOUR SERVICE, DEARIE...

AND THEN THERE'S ME. THEY CALL ME "ELDER", BECAUSE I'M THE BOSS! WE DON'T PLAY GAMES AROUND HERE...

ONE LITTLE MISTAKE AND YOU'RE DEAD... GET ME?

I DON'T MAKE MISTAKES.

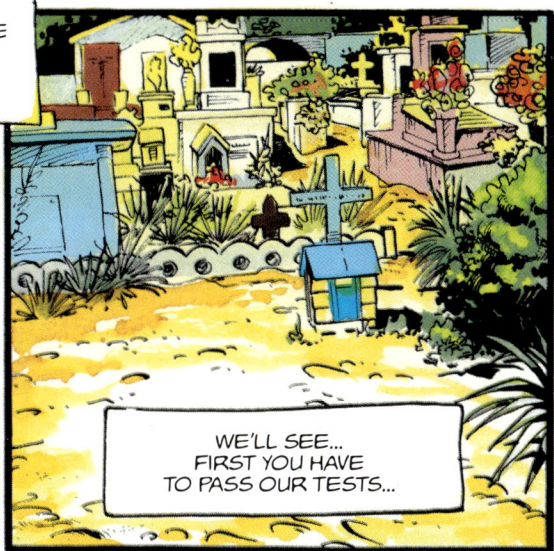

WE'LL SEE... FIRST YOU HAVE TO PASS OUR TESTS...

CAP YOUR PISTOL WITH THIS SILENCER, JUAN...

WE NEED YOU TO TAKE CARE OF WIRE'S KILLER... LET'S SEE IF YOU CAN HANDLE IT...

FETCH ME THAT SCUM, TUTTI-FRUTTI!

THIS OLD BITCH DARED TO STICK A KITCHEN KNIFE INTO WIRE'S BACK...

LET ME GO, MONSTERS!!

THAT EVIL MAN SLAUGHTERED MY CHILDREN...

...BECAUSE THEY SPOKE OUT AGAINST THE GOVERNMENT...

THEN HE RAPED MY NINE-YEAR-OLD DAUGHTER... I HAD TO STAB HIM, TO PUT AN END TO HIS ATROCITIES...

ENOUGH RANTING! KILL HER, JUAN.

DON'T CHOOSE THE WRONG PATH, MY SON... DON'T SIGN YOUR SOUL OVER TO THESE DEMONS... YOU'RE NOT ONE OF THEM... YOU'RE A HUMAN BEING! REFUSE TO OBEY THEM!

OBEY GOD'S ORDERS INSTEAD!

GOD BELIEVES IN YOU... HE'S WAITING FOR YOU...

LOOK AT THAT! HE'S CHICKENING OUT! I'LL...

HOLD ON, BIGMOUTH...

MOMMY...

?

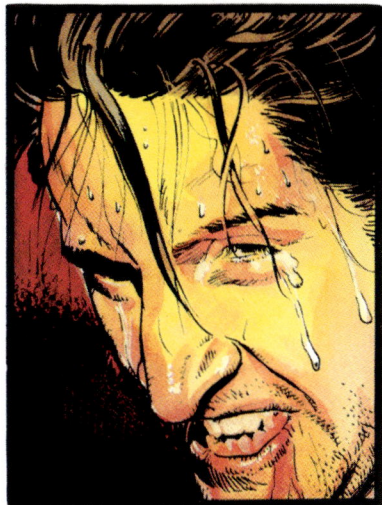

IS... IS THAT ALL?

NOW THE "GRILL"...

ONE BATTERY, TWO WIRES, AND YOU... WE'LL KEEP INCREASING THE VOLTAGE UNTIL YOU CRY "MERCY"...

TOADSTOOL'S OUR RESIDENT EXPERT... A CONNOISSEUR...

CLICK...

THE SECRET IS...

...TO SPACE OUT THE SHOCKS...

...AND MAKE SURE THE FUN LASTS...

...AND NOW, THE BEST PART... THE GENITALS...

...AS LONG AS POSSIBLE...

CRY "MERCY", IDIOT! HE'S GOING TO FRY YOUR TESTICLES!

48

HE...
HE SPIT ON ME!

OKAY, ENOUGH! JUAN SOLO JUST EARNED HIS STRIPES! CUT HIM LOOSE...

MORE THAN MOST, ANYWAY... WHAT YOU NEED NOW IS SOME NICE HOT WATER... LET'S HIT THE SHOWERS, GUYS!

LIFT HIM OFF THE FLOOR, BOYS...

WELL DONE, JUAN... YOU'VE SURE GOT GUTS...

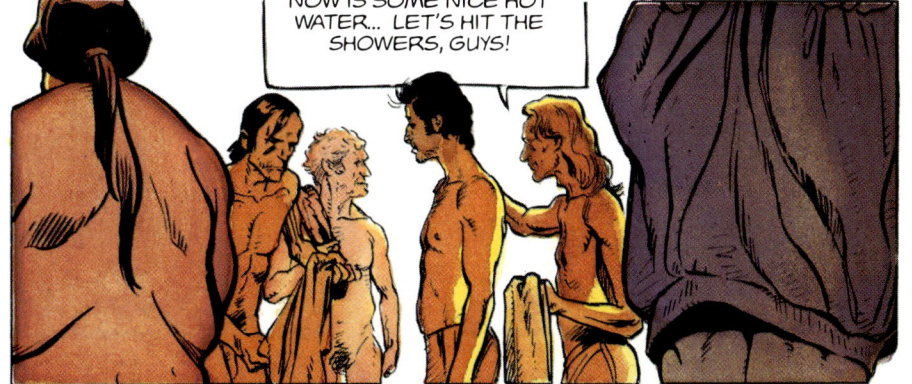

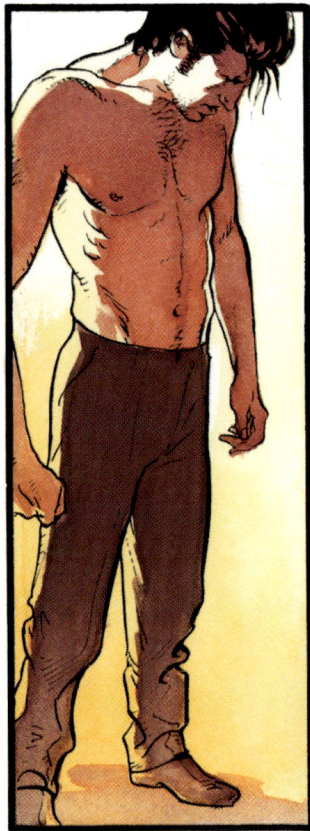

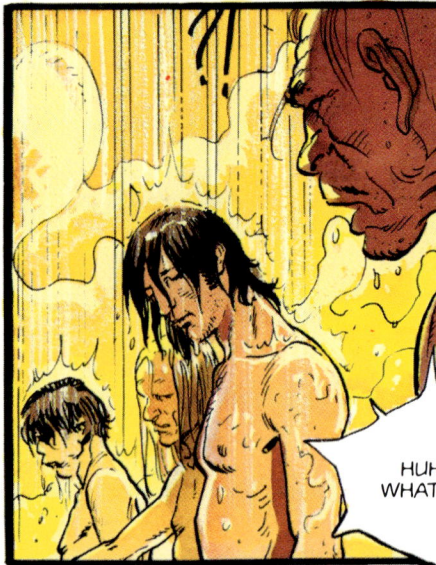

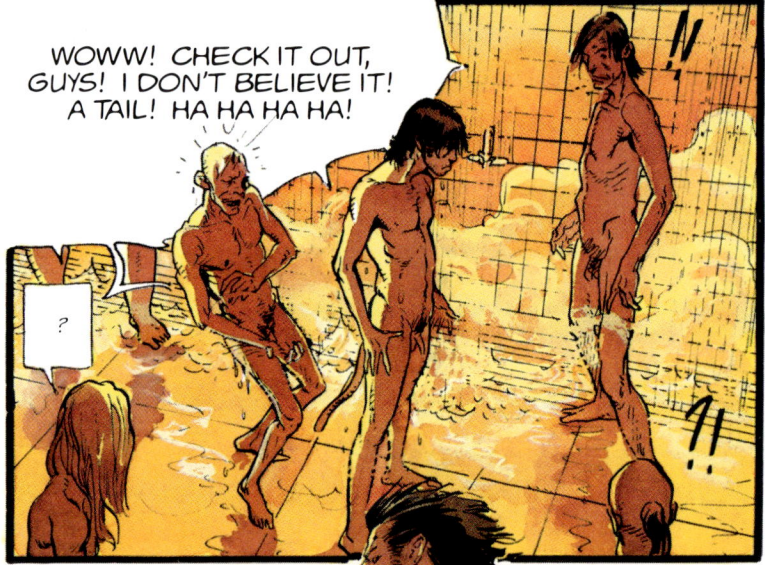

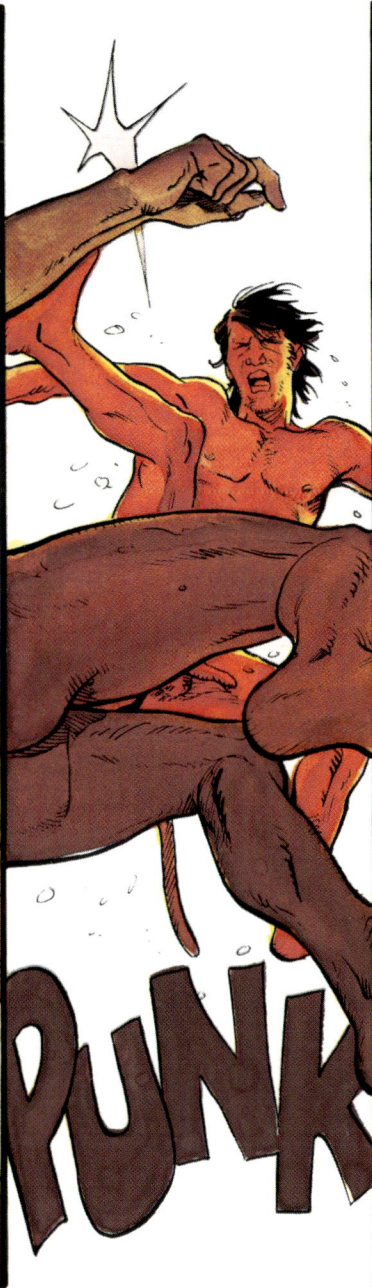

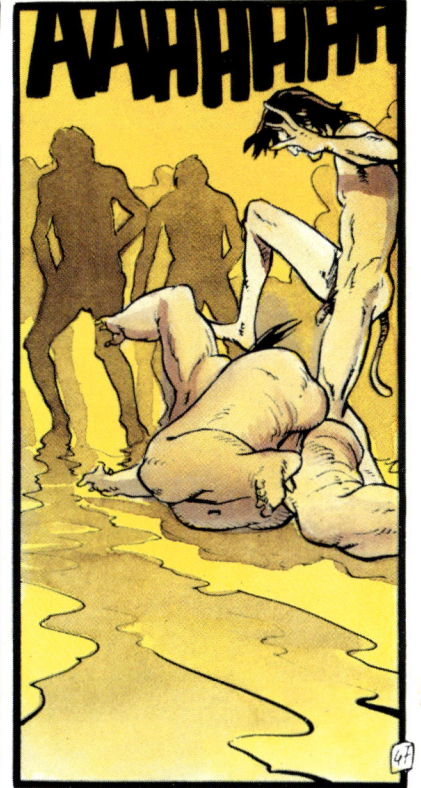

OKAY, ENOUGH! STOP FIGHTING!

HE'S ONE OF US NOW...

WE ALL HAVE OUR FLAWS...

CYCLOPS IS MISSING AN EYE... AND TOADSTOOL'S JUST A FEW INCHES AWAY FROM BEING A DWARF!

JACKAL'S UGLIER THAN A HYENA... BIGMOUTH COULD SWALLOW A BANANA LENGTHWISE...

AND BLONDIE WILL NEVER FIND THE HEROINE OF HIS DREAMS, EXCEPT FOR THE STUFF HE PUTS THROUGH HIS VEINS...

THE ONLY PLACE PINOCCHIO'S WELL-ENDOWED IS HIS NOSE... THE GREEK SMELLS LIKE A ROTTING OCTOPUS...

THE DEVIL GAVE BABYFACE THE BODY OF AN ELEPHANT AND THE BRAIN OF A FLEA...

AND FRANKENSTEIN REALLY DOES LOOK LIKE HE WAS MADE OUT OF CORPSES...

AS FOR YOU, ELDER, YOU WERE READY FOR RETIREMENT LONG AGO...

AND I'M A FAIRY, AS YOU ALL KNOW...

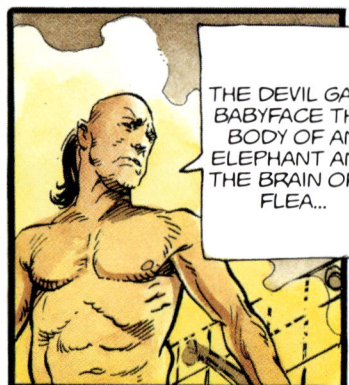

I'M LEAVING HIM IN YOUR HANDS, TUTTI-FRUTTI!

YOU CAN COUNT ON ME, ELDER.

SO LET'S MAKE PEACE WITH JUAN SOLO... AND NEVER MENTION HIS TAIL AGAIN...

YEAH, OKAY!

SURE, WE WON'T TALK TO HIM AT ALL!

NEVER!

I DON'T KNOW IF I'LL KEEP QUIET... A MAN WITH TWO TAILS SOUNDS PRETTY GOOD TO ME!

THIS WAY, JUAN... I'LL SHOW YOU YOUR ROOM, THE TV ROOM, AND EVERYTHING ELSE... DON'T FROWN... YOU'RE BETTER OFF WITHOUT THOSE GUYS TALKING TO YOU... THEY ONLY SAY DUMB THINGS ANYWAY...

52

EL GENERAL IS DRIVING ME CRAZY!... HE KNOWS HOW DANGEROUS IT IS FOR A PUBLIC FIGURE LIKE MYSELF TO VENTURE OUT INTO THE STREETS...

...BUT HE INSISTS ON HAVING HIS PRIME MINISTER BY HIS SIDE WHEN HE INAUGURATES THE VILLA HE'S GIVING TO HIS MISTRESS, THAT SLUT OF A FOLK-SINGER...

I'M RISKING MY NECK FOR HER BIG TITS...

GOLD-DIGGING WENCH...

STAY CALM, SIR... NOTHING CAN HAPPEN... YOU'RE WELL-PROTECTED...

WELL-PROTECTED?! WHAT IF SOMEONE DROPS A BOMB ON ME FROM A HELICOPTER, OR A BALCONY?

ANYONE COULD SHOOT ANY MOMENT FROM A WINDOW IN ONE OF THESE BUILDINGS... HIRED KILLERS RENT THEMSELVES CHEAP!

SANDRINEZ, EVERYWHERE! CLUTTERING UP THE LANDSCAPE! AND WHY ALL THIS PUBLICITY? BECAUSE HE WANTS TO BE PRIME MINISTER, THAT'S WHY! HE WANTS TO TAKE MY PLACE... AND I'M STANDING IN HIS WAY...

EL GENERAL DOESN'T TRUST ANYONE BUT ME... I DO EVERYTHING FOR HIM... I EVEN BUY TAMPAX FOR HIS MISTRESS! SANDRINEZ WILL NEVER GET ME OUT! HE'LL HAVE TO KILL ME FIRST!

HE'LL USE ANY MEANS HE CAN TO ELIMINATE ME...

WHAT CAN I DO? I DON'T WANT TO DIE... I DON'T WANT... ARGGH! MY STOMACH CRAMPS ARE BACK!

I KNOW A CURE FOR YOUR FEAR, BOSS...

IT'S NOT FEAR THAT'S BOTHERING ME, YOU FOOL... IT'S DEATH!

HOW CAN I LIVE WHEN I'M CONSTANTLY UNDER THREAT OF ATTACK? NOBODY'S INVULNERABLE!

THAT'S WHAT I'M TALKING ABOUT, BOSS...

STOP THE CAR AT THE NEXT INTERSECTION, BIGMOUTH!

?

WHERE ARE YOU GOING, JUAN? IF YOU LEAVE YOUR POST, DON'T BOTHER COMING BACK!

YOU CAN'T LEAVE ME IN THE MIDDLE OF DANGER!

KLAK!

DON'T WORRY, BOSS. I'M JUST GOING TO GET YOUR CURE.

!?...

VRRAAARRR

AT PARTY HEADQUARTERS...

SANDIRINEZ

EEEEEKKK!

KLACK!

OWW!

THAT HURT, YOU MURDERER!

OH! EXCUSE ME, MR. MINISTER... I'M VERY SORRY...

IF A LITTLE NEEDLE HURTS SO MUCH, WHAT ABOUT A KNIFE-THRUST? OR A BULLET... A BOMB! JUST THINK OF IT...

TRY TO RELAX, MR. MINISTER... I'VE GIVEN YOU A POWERFUL TRANQUILIZER...

THAT AND A FEW VALIUMS, AND YOU'LL FEEL MUCH BETTER SOON... YOU'LL SEE...

53

JUST THINK, DOC... I TRAVELED FOR MILES THROUGH SLUM NEIGHBORHOODS TO MAKE AN APPEARANCE AT THAT DAMNED OPENING...

!...

UHH... NOT MORE THAN ONE EVERY SIX HOURS, MR. MINISTER...

...AND THE SAME AGAIN ON THE TRIP BACK!

THE GENERAL ABSOLUTELY REQUIRED MY PRESENCE... AT HIS LITTLE WHORE'S HOUSEWARMING PARTY... "A SIMPLE VILLA IN A SIMPLE NEIGHBORHOOD"! SIMPLE, MY ASS! YOU SHOULD HAVE SEEN IT, DOC! MARBLE SHITTERS AND FURNITURE IMPORTED FROM FRANCE... CLIMATE-CONTROL, BUBBLE-BATH, SILVER DISHES...

THE "SAVIOR OF THE PEOPLE" SMUGGLES LITERALLY TONS OF GOLD INGOTS OUT OF THE COUNTRY AND INTO HIS SWISS BANK ACCOUNT...

AFTER I ARRIVED, I HAD TO LISTEN TO TWENTY TANGOS FROM THAT FOUL-MOUTHED SLUT... A SHAMELESS HUSSY WHOSE ONLY TALENT...

...CONSISTS OF PERFORMING IN A MINI-DRESS, WITH NO UNDERWEAR...

SANDRIN

...WHICH IS PRECISELY WHY THE GENERAL MADE HER DANCE ON THE TABLE, AS HE LEANED BACK IN HIS CHAIR AND LET HIS LECHEROUS GAZE LINGER OVER HER GRINDING BEAVER LIKE IT WAS THE IMMACULATE CUNT OF THE VIRGIN MARY!

AS FOR ME, I HAD THE DUBIOUS HONOR OF SITTING BY HIS RIGHT SIDE... BUT ALL THE BANNERS ONLY HAD PORTRAITS OF HIM AND... SANDRINEZ!... THAT SNAKE HAS ALMOST WON HIM OVER... NOW THE ONLY OBSTACLE STANDING IN HIS WAY IS... ME!

I THINK YOU NEED A STRONGER DOSE, MR. MINISTER...

KNOCK KNOCK!

EXCUSE ME, BOSS... CAN I COME IN?

JUA...JUAN SOLO? YOU BASTARD! WHERE HAVE YOU BEEN? YOU LEFT ME IN A TIME OF DANGER!

YOU CRAZY, STUPID FOOL! I DIDN'T ORDER ANY OF THAT! NEVER ACT ON YOUR OWN INITIATIVE AGAIN! AROUND HERE, I DO THE THINKING...

...AND ELDER GIVES THE ORDERS.

STILL... TAKE THIS, YOU CERTAINLY EARNED IT.

PARDON ME, BOSS... BUT IF JUAN MADE A MISTAKE, WHY ARE YOU REWARDING HIM?

LET'S BE HONEST! HIS ONLY MISTAKE WAS THINKING BETTER THAN YOU... AM I RIGHT?

HE UNDERSTANDS THAT IN WARTIME, ATTACK IS OFTEN THE STRONGEST DEFENSE! THIS MAN IS AS EFFICIENT AND BRAVE AS A DEMON!

WELL THEN, YOU SHOULD KEEP IT FROM GETTING BIGGER... SHOW HIM WHO'S THE STRONGER MAN, IF YOU THINK IT'S YOU.

YOU SHOULD GIVE HIM MORE IMPORTANT MISSIONS...

...HE'S NOT LIKE US... HE'S GOT A BIG HEAD...

HAH! THESE OLD FISTS CAN STILL POUND HIM INTO DIRT!

TAKE CARE, BOSS...

HMM... NOW THAT I'D LIKE TO SEE...

JUST SAY WHEN, BOSS...

61

JUAN SOLO, DO YOU DARE CHALLENGE ELDER IN UNARMED COMBAT? NO TIME LIMIT... THE LOSER IS WHOEVER CRIES "MERCY" FIRST...

DARE? I WOULD DARE CHALLENGE GOD HIMSELF...

...BUT ELDER'S MY BOSS. I FOLLOW HIS ORDERS...

IF YOU WIN, IT'LL BE YOU GIVING THE ORDERS...

AND IF HE LOSES?

BECAUSE I WON'T CRY "MERCY"...

THEN...

...I'LL HAVE TO KILL YOU...

I WON'T LOSE...

...I'LL HAVE TO KILL YOU...

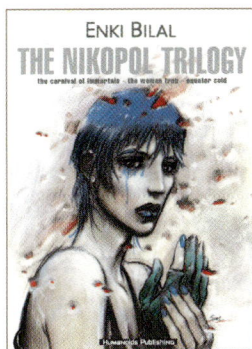

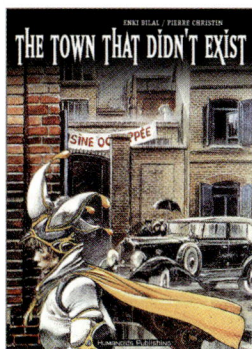

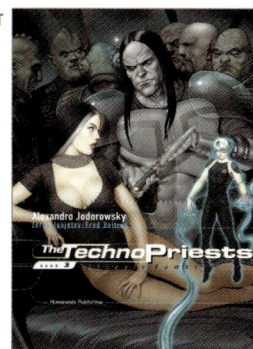

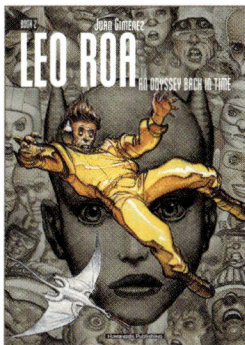

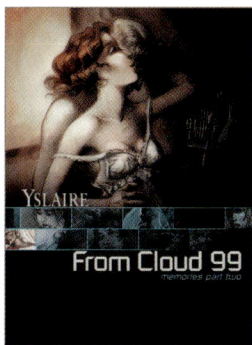

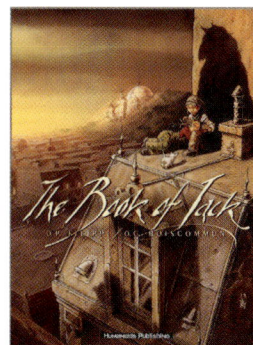

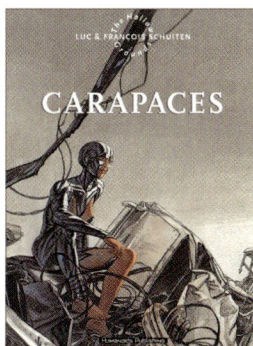

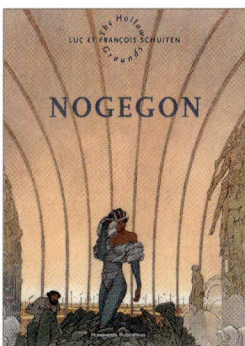